This fairy tale is dedicated to
Caroline and Jack

Without their patience and persistence
it would not have come into being

The
Magical
Master Snowman
and the
Black Dragon

A multi-layered fairy tale for all ages

Written and Illustrated by
Josephine Chaudoin Harrison

National Library of Canada Cataloguing in Publication Data
Harrison, Josephine Chaudoin, 1932-

The magical master snowman and the black dragon
ISBN 1-894694-12-0

I. Title.

PZ7 H249 Ma 2002   j813'.6   C2002-910881-0

Illustrations: Josephine Chaudoin Harrison
Manuscript enhancement: Michael Tayles
Editing: Susan Hooey
Proofreading: Neall Calvert
Photography: Dennis Cannon
Cover and book design: Fiona Raven

First Printing September 2002
Printed by Hemlock Printers Ltd.
Vancouver, Canada

Granville Island Publishing
Suite 212–1656 Duranleau
Vancouver, BC, Canada V6H 3S4
Tel 604-688-0320 Toll-free 1-877-688-0320
www.granvilleislandpublishing.com

Acknowledgements

It is not possible to write about the many people who shared in the weaving of a tapestry that became this book. These experiences have greatly enriched my life.

It was Helen May, an Early Childhood Educator, who inspired me to create this tale. She related to me her life in Africa—her remembrances of her father telling her bedtime stories in Zulu, and her Zulu nanny crooning lullabies about the day's events. Thank you, Helen.

Thank you to Naomi Serrano, PhD, Family and Child Therapist, for your inner strength and sincere support.

Thank you Jo Blackmore of Granville Island Publishing, for all your help through the publishing and marketing process.

Warmest thanks to Fiona Raven and Susan Hooey. Susan, your editing was truly objective and creative. I appreciated your dedication and support. It was a pleasure to work with you and Michael Tayles, whose enthusiasm and brilliance helped to light up this story.

Fiona, your calmness in troubled waters and excellent sense of design has enriched the artwork.

Thanks also to Petra Robinson, a guiding hand through the complexities of printing this book.

It was a privilege to work with you all. Thank you, from my heart.

Josephine Chaudoin Harrison

Author's Note:

The dictionary meaning of snowman is *dweller in the snow*. This fairy tale transforms the dwellers in the snow into guardians of humanity, both male and female in one being. The word *he* is used in place of *it* or *he/she*.

Preface

This tale tumbled out one wintry November night in 2000, on a little island in the Pacific Northwest called Bowen Island. It was completed in New Zealand with the help of the Master Snowman, who appeared to the writer with some necessary details for the last chapter.

Contents

1   The Snowman in the Meadow   1

2   Magical Realities   9

3   A Place Called Nada   17

4   A Perfect Friend   25

5   The Rose Planet   33

6   Timeless Adventure   57

7   Eyesore Island   61

8   The Challenge   71

9   The World is Transformed   83

The Snowman
in the Meadow

Totter-Grass, a small village in the high country of Wonder-Peak Mountain, sat perched on a little hill overlooking an expanse of meadow. The forest beyond sheltered Totter-Grass from frequent storms. The winters were cold with plenty of sun and fluffy, sticky snow. This winter there was a well-trodden path from Totter-Grass to the meadow where the village children had taken several days to build a magnificent snowman that stood over six feet tall.

The sun shone on Polly's golden curls as the children raced through the snow to find bits and pieces for the finishing touches: arms and hands of dead branches, twigs at the end looking like fingers; eyebrows and smiling mouth of twigs too. They selected his eyes, nose and buttons from a pile of rock chips that the wind had uncovered. Polly's kind-hearted older brother, George, taller, with tousled hair

and piercing brown eyes, brought a box from their Dad's
shed for Polly to stand on to reach the snowman's head.
Julie, Polly's best friend, handed her a black top hat and
then the snowman was complete! Oh no, not quite —
George reached into the box to pull out an old pair of boots
and called out, "We need these too!"

He turned at the sound of distant voices and laughed
with delight, "Hey Polly, all the villagers have heard about
the snowman and are turning out to see our masterpiece!"

Polly's face lit up with a big smile. "Even Gran'pa's
coming!" she cried.

As the crowd approached, *oohs* and *ahs* were heard.

At dusk, everyone made their way back to the village.
Polly turned to look at the snowman in the evening light. It
glowed as stars peeped through a darkening sky. Polly
waved and, to her surprise, the snowman appeared to wave
back. By the time they arrived home, the moon was bright
and stars filled the sky.

That evening, Polly sat in front of the wood fire beside
her father's chair. His large feet rested on a puff. Mother
came in from the kitchen carrying hot chocolate just as a
storm warning blared from the TV. Polly leapt to the window
and squinted through the blackness, wishing she could see
to the meadow and the snowman. Her brow furled in worry.

Her thoughts were brought back to the present by a
nudge from George as he handed her a steaming mug from

the tray, "Here's your hot chocolate, Sis."

"Shush, George," said Dad. "Listen!"

The anchor woman reported that the Crashem Company were going to clear-cut the old forest near Totter-Grass. Polly cried, "That's us! That's our forest!"

"Children," said Mum in a low voice, "we will do everything we can to ensure that doesn't happen. Now off to bed."

George and Polly slowly made their way upstairs, trying to delay the inevitable bedtime for as long as possible. Mum smiled affectionately and indulgently at their snail's pace and followed behind. Before closing the blue and white striped curtains in her bedroom, Polly looked out of the window and saw the stars still shining brightly. As she hopped into bed, Mum entered the room to read her a bedtime story and give her a good-night kiss.

"Mum, the beautiful phoenix in the story is real, isn't it?" asked Polly.

"As real as the fairies in the forest that take care of the wonderful old trees," Mum replied, "—trees that give homes to the birds, animals and insects," Polly interjected.

Mum picked up Polly's favorite doll, Dimpsee, a floppy rag doll with braided hair, and tucked the beloved companion in beside her, giving them both a butterfly kiss goodnight.

Later that night, as the wind rattled the windows, Polly awoke from a dream. Sitting up and clasping Dimpsee, she gasped, "Is there a fairy in the room? Do you see one, Dimpsee?" She climbed out of bed and went to the window. "It's very dark and the stars are gone," she whispered. "We had better check on the snowman."

As Polly tiptoed downstairs whilst imagining herself the size of an elf, Dimpsee slipped out of her hand. "Oh, Dimpsee!" Polly cried, suddenly feeling very alone as she fumbled in the dark hallway for the doll. Polly put on her warmest sweater, a jacket, warm boots and her beret with the pom-pom on top. Clutching Dimpsee closely, she opened the door very quietly and stepped into the cold night air as a gust of wind whirled around her.

Polly crunched through the snow in the direction of the meadow. The wind howled in the trees and she realised she had missed the tracks to the meadow. She was deep in the forest. She caught a brief glimpse of a dark shape lurking in the shadows, watching. Polly's heart beat wildly with fear. She whispered to Dimpsee, tucked inside her jacket, "Let's go this way."

With her head down to protect her face from the cutting wind, Polly didn't see the same dark shape crouching between the trees. Just then a large old tree swayed—there was a fierce cracking as a huge branch fell towards her. At that moment the moon shot through the clouds. A ray shone on the dark shape. 'Could it be a dragon?' This final thought flashed across her mind before the falling branch crushed Polly and Dimpsee deep into the snow, leaving no trace except her brightly colored beret with the pom-pom on top.

2 Magical Realities

When Polly opened her eyes she found herself lying in cosy, soft, white stuff that seemed to be snow, but was not cold like snow. She sat up, looked around and saw the snowman from the meadow.

'I'm glad to see you are all right,' she said with a sigh of relief.

He smiled and helped her to her feet. A light-filled brightness beamed all around. Polly felt happy and free. She remembered the storm and tried to recall what had happened. 'Where am I? No meadow? A live snowman!' she cried. She became aware that she was on an iceberg which was floating in the air like a flying ship. When she peered over the edge of the craft she saw a large gathering in the woods and exclaimed, 'Everyone from the village is here!' As she looked more closely she was startled to see herself there, below, under the fallen tree.

A woodsman had found her body under the broken branch. Her parents and George were crying. Straining to see more, and forgetting her precarious position, she leaned even further and slipped off the iceship. As she started to fall she discovered, to her amazement, that she could fly! She flew to her family but nobody seemed to notice her. 'I am just fine, not hurt at all,' she tried to tell them.

Then Polly soared to the meadow to see if her snowman was still there because, curiously, the one on the iceship looked just like him. Although a bit battered by the storm,

his hat askew, the meadow snowman towered majestically in the exact spot where they had made him. He was surrounded by the village children, who didn't see her arrive. They were talking about her. "How awful to get lost in a storm like that," sobbed Julie. "Polly should never have gone out. I will miss her so much."

'I wonder why nobody can see me!' said Polly in bewilderment. 'Could I be dead? I don't feel dead, I feel terrific.' Polly then realized that she had another body that couldn't be seen. The children gradually wandered away. When she was alone, something extraordinary happened. As Polly looked at the snowman his eyes twinkled and a live snowman stepped out of the snow body! 'Oh!' she exclaimed, 'You have more than one body too!' He nodded and Polly suddenly had the impression that he was speaking silently in her head. He said, 'Everyone has another body that is not usually visible but is always a part of them.' The snowman continued silently, 'This is your real body that lasts forever.'

Polly asked him, 'Where am I?'

'I'll show you,' he answered.

Together they floated up to the iceship. Polly felt safe and secure again.

A Place
Called Nada

The iceship floated through space under a rainbow arch
and stopped. 'Hello. I'm Polly,' she greeted the snowman as
she stepped off the iceship. The snowman smiled, '*You* can
call mc Mcadow.' Polly soon discovered that everyone called
him Master as a way of showing enormous respect. In his
top hat, Meadow Master, also known as "Kindly One," was
senior to twelve snowmen masters. They were recognised
by their hats. Second to Meadow was a snowman named
Keeptothepath in a mortarboard that he had worn at

Cambridge University in an Earth life. The third snowman, Rajputwill, wore a magnificent turban. Another had an exquisite velvet hat with an ostrich feather worn at the French court. Motherbell wore a blue hat decked with pink roses and Rushalong a check flat cap. Other snowmen wore a Mexican straw hat, a cowboy hat and a Chinese coolie hat.

'What *is* this place?' Polly asked. 'It's Nada,' replied Meadow Master. 'Nada?' Polly repeated. 'Yes. Nothingness,' said the magical master snowman.

There were many children in this place beyond Earth. Polly noticed that they were from all over the world. Motherbell, together with Inner Peace, looked after them. On Nada, the children understood one another because they could open windows that showed each other's Earth lives. One of the children opened a window to reveal how he had fallen into a river near his home and drowned. 'Could this be why some people are afraid to swim?' asked Polly. Meadow Master nodded.

'Do we have more than one life? Is that possible?' asked Polly. 'Many lives. That is how you become the embodiment of goodness,' replied Meadow Master, bowing his head slightly.

In Nada, thoughts were three-dimensional pictures. Bodies were weightless and everyone flew from one place to another. Communication was silent. Time did not exist, just rhythm. Polly found it easy to accept this way of life.

In this heightened awareness, the children became more mature in their thinking and were less attached to the past and therefore free to move on to new adventures and understanding. Here, everything they thought or imagined instantly appeared. Polly found it could be very crowded until she got her confused thoughts under control.

Thinking of happy times with her family, she visualised a little cabin near clear running water with trees, mountains, meadows full of flowers, birds singing and her brother George befriending the cottontails with carrots. 'Just like our favorite cabin in the mountains,' Polly marvelled as the pictures in her head appeared in front of her.

When her thoughts got too muddled, the snowman called Rushalong, wearing his check flat cap, appeared to help her. He brushed up those thoughts that were no longer needed and swept them into piles called *tumblebundles*.

Then they just disappeared. 'It must be some sort of magic,' concluded Polly.

Rushalong winked at her.

While relating her experiences in her last life, Polly's mind went back to that day in Totter-Grass when Meadow Master stepped out of his snow body. She wondered, 'How could that happen?' The magic word *love* popped into her mind and she realised that her genuine love for him was the reason why he could help her. Polly also knew that her experience was not unique. Other snowmen masters came alive to help children, though not always in a snowman's body. Windows onto Earth opened and Polly watched a little girl being saved from a fire in her home by the energy of a cross of light created by a snowman master. The child was protected by rays shining into the room where nobody knew she was trapped. Polly was so in awe that she was speechless.

The snowmen understood the problems on Earth. Remarkably, they also knew how to solve them. However, to do so, they needed the help of people from all over the world. The snowmen were patient and very kind and somehow they were like fathers and mothers all in one. 'But none have quite the special energy of Meadow Master,' discerned Polly. She inquired how they became snowmen masters, where they came from, and how they knew so much. Meadow Master replied, 'One begins by believing in the goodness of one's self and the goodness of others. Then it is a long apprenticeship of practice and acquiring experience and wisdom. Polly remembered the Crashem Company and said, 'But not everyone's good.' Meadow Master sighed, 'Everyone is good deep, deep within.'

Color Collages

The Stars live in a sea of energy.

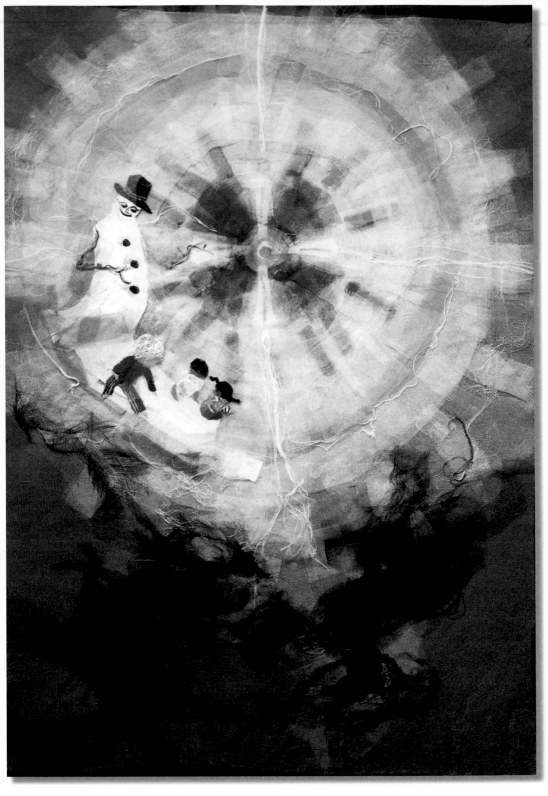

A cosmic cross appeared, seeming to dissolve the pollution with its rays.

Color Collages

		page
1	The Snowman	2
2	A Dark Shape	31
3	The Stars	36
4	A Cosmic Cross	60

4   *A Perfect Friend*

On Earth, Polly had believed that help came through prayer. On Nada, Meadow Master was always there if she needed help. When she had a strange feeling and thought, 'Something is happening to my family,' almost instantly Meadow Master appeared on his iceship. Polly jumped aboard and together they sailed through space to the clouds over Earth. There below she saw the pretty little church her family attended. A menacing dark shadow prowled outside, yet nobody seemed to notice it. 'Perhaps the bright light inside prevents the entry of such evil,' she thought.

Many people were gathered. Polly wondered what the occasion could be, so she flew down and passed through the wall to find out.

It was not the familiar service. Flowers filled every available space. Some people were wearing black and the atmosphere felt sorrowful. Polly watched from the front aisle. Her family was in the middle of the front row singing her favorite hymn, *Above the Bright Blue Sky*. 'Someone has died,' Polly realised. She trembled as she approached the altar rail. A circle of light was shining above the flower-covered coffin. 'Who has died and what is that circle of light?' she asked uneasily. To her surprise, the circle of light spoke to her in her head, 'If you don't know what I am or who I am, you do not know yourself. But if you ask me, I will tell you.'

'What are you, then?' asked Polly bravely.

'I am the real you. I am your soul,' the light resonated.

'Then why are you over there and not here inside me?' countered Polly.

'Because I can get your attention over here,' the light chuckled.

Polly remembered her parents explaining that the soul is in the heart. Feeling very mixed up, she overheard Gran'pa say, 'We will miss Polly very much.' The funeral was for her! Nada was not a dream! The light glittered in agreement and explained lovingly that only part of her was dead.

'You, the *real* Polly, is very alive. You are a circle of light that is everywhere.' Polly liked this idea and thought of herself as a light. The circle of light merged with her. Startled at its disappearance, she wondered, 'Now where has it gone?'

'I'm here inside you,' called the light as it floated out again.

Polly, who was feeling quite human in spite of being dead, asked matter-of-factly, 'What can I call you?' Before the light could reply, the name of her cherished doll *Dimpsee*, popped into her head. Dimpsee, the rag doll with a dimple in its chin.

As the funeral service ended, Polly noticed that everyone had a circle of light. Some circles were very bright, others could hardly be seen. She called these lights *dimplights*. The light usually appeared just above the head and glowed all around the person. Her parents and brother had bright lights shining in their hearts. Although they looked sad, Polly was certain they knew that she was not really gone. This reassured her. Polly floated over to her Mum, whose eyelashes were wet with tears, and gave her a butterfly kiss.

Roses and daisies filled the church with a lovely fragrance. The choir sang a closing hymn, *Abide with Me*. Instinctively, Polly joined in. The group gradually departed. Outside, the ominous presence still lurked. A rotten stench emanated from the gruesome creature. Polly was terrified. She sought Dimpsee's counsel. Not glowing as brightly as before, Dimpsee said warily, 'The energy of fear is like a hard shell that blocks the light from reaching us.' Polly tried to dispel the fearful feeling. Dimpsee continued, 'The dark shape is the Black Dragon, who has become a great danger to humanity. Without understanding the consequences,

humanity created this monster out of selfishness and greed.'

'Why is it here at my funeral?' demanded Polly.

'The dragon caused your accident and made the forest near Totter-Grass appear dangerous in order to diminish the community's effectiveness in saving those old trees. It is trying to influence your parents with its sinister energy because they are against the clearing of the forest. Fortunately, your parents are too aware to be intimidated like that,' said Dimpsee confidently.

Polly still had questions in her heart as she flew up into the blue sky back to the iceship. 'How does selfishness and greed create a monster?' she wanted to know.

Meadow Master replied, 'Wanting more and more is like an unquenchable thirst. Desires can never be satisfied and this creates a negative energy that alters people's attitudes and prevents them from expressing their inner beauty.'

'So what can we do about that wicked dragon?' Polly asked fervently.

'Sharing is the way,' said Meadow Master calmly as the iceship floated away. The snowman embraced her and in spite of all that had happened, she felt at peace again.

5   *The Rose Planet*

Polly was eager for more experiences and adventures in
her new life on Nada, so when Meadow Master arrived on
his iceship with two children, Pip and Lu, to take them all
on a journey, she was excited. With her natural warmth and
friendliness, she introduced herself. Lu, smiling shyly,
asked, 'How did you get here?' Polly described her accident
and the way in which the snowman in the meadow came
alive. Fascinated in her own quiet way by Polly's story, Lu
opened a window that showed herself on a refugee ship that
sank on the way to North America. 'How awful!' said Polly
compassionately. They turned to Pip, whose smile went
from ear to ear. His window opened to Africa and they saw
his Earth body deformed by starvation. He had died from
malnutrition. Polly shuddered to see the suffering these
children endured. She realised how fortunate she
had been.

Planet Earth disappeared in a haze of pollution as the iceship glided away through space. Soon, a beautiful rose-colored light surrounded them. In the light, another planet became visible. A ring of rose petals swirled around it like a veil. As the iceship passed through the petals, the children began to see clearly.

Fine sand covered the surface. It was a mountainous landscape without vegetation. Vibrant golden Stars welcomed them as the iceship landed on a plateau. Living in a sea of energy, these Stars formed beautiful shapes and radiated colors that Polly had never seen before. They too communicated silently.

The Stars turned toward a group of shapes on the hillside. 'These are our homes. We create any form we need from pure energy and color it for different tasks.' Polly noticed large saucer-like objects hovering over the mountains. The Stars satisfied her curiosity by telling her that these were used for travel to other planets. 'We have visited Earth,' they divulged, 'to observe the pollution and discarded *hardware* left in space. You've seen some of our art work. We understand you call them *crop circles*.'

'What a wonderful way to awaken humans to the possibility that other beings live in space!' exclaimed Polly.

'The atmosphere here is alive with ideas and opportunities to learn,' the Stars stated. 'On the Rose Planet, you will prepare yourselves for life on Earth.'

Polly, Lu, Pip and the group of Stars who welcomed them were transported in a dome of color to an enchanted valley. They saw rose slopes and sparkling, dancing colors in the shape of flowers. A pink light illuminated everything. The energy was dynamic. Some students were already seated on the soft sand facing Meadow Master, who was about to give a lesson.

Meadow Master taught in such an interesting way. To help the students understand the lessons, he opened windows onto Earth and sometimes disclosed a past life to clarify a point. He illustrated the teachings by using dimplights shaped like gingerbread men so that his words came alive to the students. They saw a dimplight in the body of a boy in one life, and in a girl in the next. Polly was not sure how she felt about that! Windows opened within Polly to reveal her own lives as a sequence of story pictures. She realised that certain things continue from one life to the next and that if we care about others as much as we care about ourselves, many problems melt away.

Meadow Master grinned mischievously. Suddenly the dimplights became sharing and selfish thoughts on boomerangs. 'Thoughts and actions always return to their

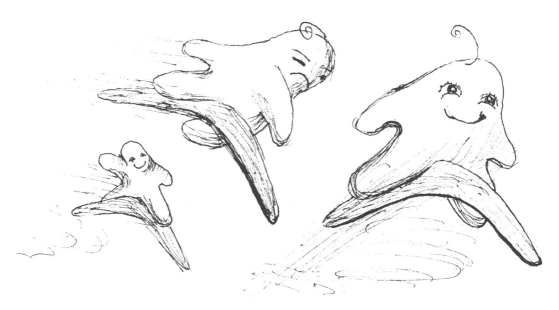

sender,' said Meadow Master. A selfish thought on a boomerang hissing, 'Me, me, me,' whizzed over Polly's head. She ducked and squealed, 'No time to be bored in this school!' The children laughed.

With a twinkle in his eye, Meadow Master opened a window to show millions of stars in the universe

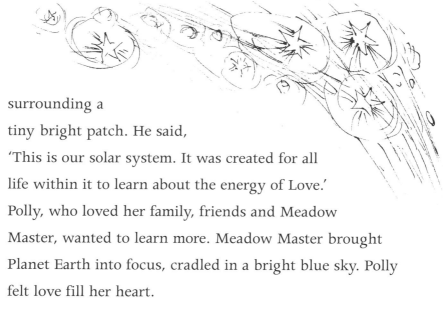

surrounding a
tiny bright patch. He said,
'This is our solar system. It was created for all
life within it to learn about the energy of Love.'
Polly, who loved her family, friends and Meadow
Master, wanted to learn more. Meadow Master brought
Planet Earth into focus, cradled in a bright blue sky. Polly
felt love fill her heart.

Then the picture changed to Earth with grey smog swirling around it, fish dying in the rivers and sea, birds and insects killed from insecticides, animals inflicted with terrible diseases, forests destroyed and humans suffering from strange illnesses. Polly perceived that the Earth was dying. 'Oh! The Earth needs to be loved too!' she wept. Meadow Master's serene gaze met hers. 'Now you're on the way,' he whispered.

Polly then knew that everything needs to be loved.
Meadow Master continued, 'In the last two thousand
years, Mother Earth has been neglected.

The balance of life is delicate, and what affects one, affects all.' With a sweep of his long twig fingers, Meadow Master drew a circle in the sand. 'This is the circle of life. Earth is the Great Mother, nurturing life, and love is the energy that

holds everything together.' As Meadow Master spoke, Polly saw baby dimplights like fairies and devas, and what looked like angels beaming wings of energy. 'How beautiful and wonderful,' she murmured.

Meadow Master began the next lesson with a picture of a dimplight swinging to Earth on a cord. The parents could not care for it, so the baby was adopted by a family who joyfully welcomed this wonderful gift.

Meadow Master held the world in his hand, selected an area, and then opened windows. 'In this part of the world, war has destroyed many villages and much farmland,' he informed them. 'Children and adults work very hard for food, clothing and shelter. In some countries, children work

long hours, often under harsh working conditions, to
provide products for businesses in other parts of the world.
Exploiting child labor is inhuman. Many families do not
have enough money for food or a home. This causes
unhappiness. Some of them turn to drugs to escape the

pain. They think that drug highs are Nada. But they are deluded and trapped in the space between Earth and Nada where nothing gets better. It's all make-believe and wishful thinking,' lamented Meadow Master.

In the midst of such despair, the ebony shadow of the Black Dragon loomed threateningly. Polly shuddered, 'That dragon was at my funeral!'

'Yes Polly,' replied Meadow Master, 'It is everywhere.'

Then the children observed two directors of Bonkers and Tops, a multimillion-dollar department store chain, discussing money. Polly couldn't understand why they were not discussing ways to share their wealth.

Meadow Master, who knew everyone's thoughts, addressed her unspoken concern saying, 'Mr. Boxit made millions making cardboard packing boxes. He was

successful and satisfied, and only became generous after a
visit to India where he saw a little boy and his family living
on a street in Calcutta in discarded Boxit boxes. Hearing this
story, the director of his company, Agnes Upover, was
inspired to form a donation-based organisation called FHLO,
Family Homes for Little Ones.'

'When even a few wealthy people consider others and share their resources, the world becomes a better place,' Meadow Master said optimistically.

Another scene opened showing Samuel Goodmany sitting at an enormous desk in Los Angeles writing a

ten-million-dollar check
to provide materials and
labor to dig wells for
villages without water in
Africa and other
disadvantaged parts of
the world. He did not
want children to die from
dirty, infectious drinking
water.

These positive choices and acts of generosity made a deep impression on Polly.

Polly tapped her heart, 'Dimpsee, I could return to Earth to help in projects that provide clean water for villages!' Dimpsee agreed, 'It would be a rewarding life.'

Polly and her friends shared ideas about how life on Earth could be nurtured back to health and happiness. Polly eagerly anticipated her return. Ideas were tumbling from her lively imagination. She was determined to make a better world, saying, 'So much needs to be done.'

Meadow Master closed the lesson by bringing great experiences to light — what humans call miracles. Polly and Lu loved the scene of the dolphins protecting a little boy perched on a piece of wood from a refugee ship that sank in a storm. The dolphins stayed with him for days until he was rescued. The little boy did not see Meadow Master nearby on the crest of a wave, although he felt his comforting presence.

The students discovered that snowmen masters were actively involved in life on Earth. They could appear in any

guise. Polly and the students watched Meadow Master take the form of a homeless man playing a flute on a street corner to remind passers-by to have a dance in their step; and then become a mother sitting on a doorstep, caring for her child. Polly was so overwhelmed that she just managed to whisper to Meadow Master, 'Are these earthly appearances?' He nodded, 'We open closed hearts.'

Timeless
Adventure

6

The Stars announced to the students, 'You have reached a new level of learning and understanding. Now you are ready to experience a new adventure.' Two Star pilots guided them as they floated up to the entrance of a small spaceship with a flat top and windows all around. They had a good view through the pear-shaped windows. 'The universe is beautiful with all its brightly colored stars, and each planet is a player in the music of the spheres,' mused Polly.

After they had traveled past many planets, a distinctive melody sounded as they approached one called Planet Allgone. None of the students had heard it before. The Star pilot announced, 'We have entered the rhythm of Allgone.' Polly and her friends saw the shadow of the Dark Dragon. Its influence was in the form of grey shadows. The Star pilots explained, 'These shadows were caused by the selfish behavior of the citizens and quickly grew into greed. This misuse of energy eventually caused the planet so much suffering that the Allgone civilization went under the sea in an enormous volcanic eruption.'

Polly asked anxiously, 'Dimpsee, the same thing wouldn't happen on Earth today, would it?

Dimpsee reminded Polly, 'This is a timeless adventure.'

'You mean it has already happened?' Polly asked. Dimpsee smiled.

Red bubble cars suspended on fine wires arrived immediately to show the students what the planet was like before the Black Dragon corrupted the civilization. Planet Allgone was once lush with fragrant hanging gardens. Inhabitants of similar appearance to people on Earth worked happily caring for the abundant flowers and foliage. Tall, fair men and women in radiant gowns performed chants and rituals in a vast, lighted dome creating brilliant circles of light and color.

After a tour in the red bubble cars, the students returned to the spaceship. 'To complete this adventure, we are going to a planet called Aboutohappen,' said the Star pilots. Traveling there felt like a momentary journey. Instead of landing, the spaceship glided across the surface of the planet and this provided the students with a good overview. 'The people are like us,' commented Polly as they hovered over a small community. The people below waved and behaved as though they were familiar with the spaceship.

The students waved back and Polly felt a connection to the
inhabitants of Aboutohappen, as though she knew them.
She remarked, "It looks like Earth, too, but with no noise or
pollution and everyone seems to be happy and carefree.'
The students were thoughtful as they listened to the melody
of Aboutohappen become fainter. The Star pilots stated,
'This is how beautiful Earth could be if everyone worked
together.' No shadow of the Black Dragon could be seen.

'What a wonderful planet!' concluded Polly as she
waved goodbye through the window. The spaceship
ascended, destined for the Rose Planet, only a
moment away.

7 *Eyesore Island*

Meadow Master arrived on his iceship to take Polly, Lu and Pip on a journey to the core of the problems on Earth. As they approached Earth, far from the pink glow of the Rose Planet, grey pollution swirled around them. The students were glad to be in the protective light of Meadow Master even though his radiance was contained to the iceship.

Through the gloom, a cosmic cross appeared, seeming to dissolve the contamination with its rays. They approached a dark area far below and saw what looked like a volcanic island with a smoking mountain at its center. The iceship descended to the edge of the volcanic crater and stopped. The students peered into the abyss and saw a huge pile of garbage. Smoke from the rotting rubbish filled the air with a foul odor. Curious by nature, Polly wanted to see more, but Pip and Lu were cautious. Meadow Master indicated to

Polly that she could investigate, and reassured her that
Dimpsee's energy would protect her. She flew down and
landed on top of an old refrigerator. She was surrounded by
broken cars, war weapons, computers, furniture and heaps
of debris as far as she could see. Polly remembered her
parents saying, "We live in a throw-away society; nothing is
made to last any more." Polly asked incredulously, 'Is this
where it all goes?' A faintly visible Dimpsee popped out and
nodded. Polly knew that she shouldn't stay long in such an

awful place. On the far side of the crater the rock face was covered with painted slogans. Polly flew over to take a closer look. They read:

The need is greed
You can never have enough
Ugly is beautiful
I am the only one who matters

Turning away in disgust, Polly entered a large cave. She could hardly believe her eyes. A dark shape sat at a table covered with a black cloth and piled high with paper money. The shape became clearer. Polly had seen it before.

She caught her breath, 'It's the Black Dragon!' It was not aware of her presence. 'It's made of dollar bills,' Polly marveled, as she saw paper bills beneath its black scales. 'Can this be real, Dimpsee?' whispered Polly fearfully. Dimpsee popped out and nodded. 'I can hardly see you, Dimpsee!' complained Polly. 'It's because you're scared,' Dimpsee explained. 'A lot of light energy is being used to protect you.' Just then the Black Dragon whirled around to

face Polly. Its glassy eyes narrowed and it sniffed hungrily in Polly's direction.

'I'm leaving right now!' cried Polly. She fled out of the cave and saw Pip and Lu in the crater. Fearful for Polly, they had flown down to look for her. They glimpsed the dragon as Polly rushed from the cave. Back on the iceship, they felt safe with Meadow Master. 'It is good you have the courage to explore, and that Pip and Lu came down to look for you,' he said approvingly.

The students and the snowman
sailed smoothly toward the warm glow
of the Rose Planet. Meadow Master said solemnly,
'There is more to learn about the Black Dragon.'

As the iceship landed, Keeptothepath, the snowman
master wearing a mortarboard and gown, ended a lesson
with the other students. Pip, Lu and Polly were very glad to
be back on the Rose Planet. They thought a lot about what
they had seen and wondered how such a terrible monster

had come to life. Polly told the others that when she had scared thoughts, Dimpsee's light went low and the Black Dragon became aware of her. Polly speculated, 'Can being scared and having selfish, greedy thoughts attract a monster? Can a thought become a real thing?'

What adventures! 'Have we seen the past and the future as one?' wondered Polly. She tried to relate these experiences of past and future to the present. Polly reflected, 'If past and future are now, then there truly is no time.' Dimpsee replied, 'Humans first created time to measure the changing seasons of life.'

Color Collages

Meadow Master just lifted the train back onto the tracks.

Out of the ashes of a dying civilization a beautiful society

will grow —one based on love, justice and sharing.

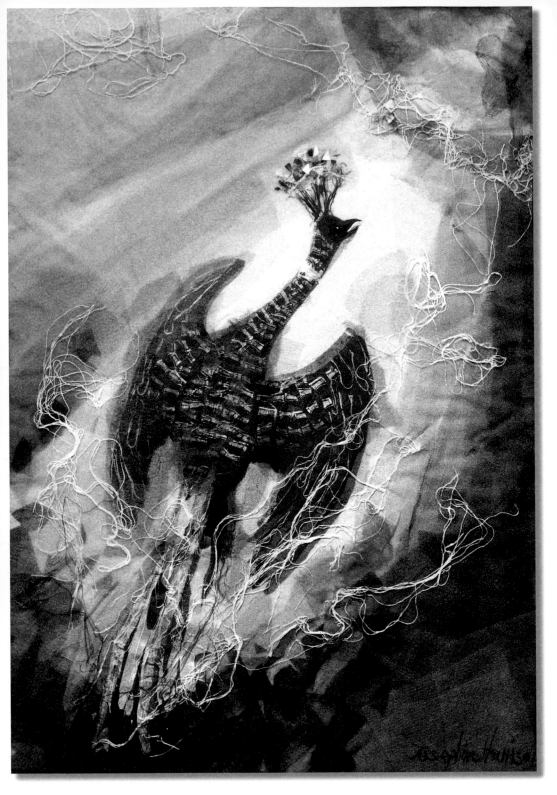

The phoenix flew upwards out of the ashes.

Color Collages

page

5   Meadow Master   76

6   Love, Justice and Sharing   80

7   The Phoenix   89

8 *The Challenge*

Meadow Master exhibited an iridescent golden egg from which a glistening dimplight hatched. It burst into the unknown, free from fear. In shape it looked rather like a gingerbread man.

Then the dimplights demonstrated that not allowing feelings to be experienced shows insincerity and not meaning what you say is dishonest. All of a sudden the sun disappeared behind a black cloud and the flowers drooped.

Next, two gingerbread
dimplights demonstrated
that allowing feelings to be
experienced leads to sincerity,
and saying what you think and
doing what you say, leads to
honesty. The sun shone brightly
and the flowers bloomed. Polly
remembered the boomerang
game with sharing and
selfish thoughts coming
back. Meadow Master instructed,
'Do not imitate others and lose your sparkle. Be yourself.'
Then the dimplights flew faster and faster, circling the
students and weaving them together in love—uniting them
as one human family.

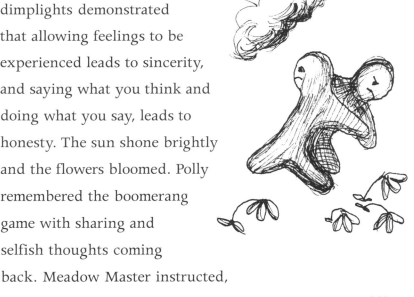

To give the students hope for the future, Meadow Master said, 'While some people value only money and things, others value creativity and serving the community. They do this whether it makes them wealthy or not.' A window opened on a skyscraper and Meadow Master foretold, 'When you return, more buildings like this one will be used for creative industries, museums and libraries.'

Then the students viewed a family living in poverty. Meadow Master said, 'See this young man with his wife and children? He invested in the money markets and made a fortune. But instead of being satisfied, then he risked everything and lost, causing his family great suffering.' Stunned, Polly asked, 'Can anyone lose money like that?'

'Yes,' replied Meadow Master. 'Observe the shadow of the Black Dragon everywhere. It feeds on selfish desire.' Another window opened and the students watched as the repulsive Black Dragon become so energized that it danced ecstatically in its cave.

The dance turned into a wild frenzy as the Black Dragon absorbed more and more of the destructive energy.

He became enormous and out of control, and charged around the world bringing about calamity — tipping over trains, bumping into airliners, breathing flames out of his nostrils causing terrible fires and upsetting the weather. The students watched with alarm as the dragon attempted to cause a terrible train crash outside London, but Meadow Master was there just in time to pull the train back from the dragon's grasp. 'People call these incidents miracles,' Meadow Master remarked. 'Sometimes we can prevent accidents, or at least save lives.'

He continued, 'The more honest and sincere everyone is with each other, the more we can be of help. This means that until everyone changes their actions to create a better world, we are limited in what we can do.'

Polly asked apprehensively, 'When will the Black Dragon be conquered? Will it be soon?'

'It's up to each of us,' acknowledged Meadow Master.

With these words, the Black Dragon began to lose its strength, it stumbled past skyscrapers, searching, hungry. Meadow Master closed the window on the horror.

Polly and Dimpsee discussed their plans for her next life. 'These plans,' Dimpsee explained, 'are like a blueprint.' Fascinated, Polly asked, 'Will I remember this blueprint?'

print?' Dimpsee replied gravely, 'When you return to Earth, the memory of all you have learnt is behind a veil. This veil is lifted through inner awareness because this keeps people in touch with their dimplights. The veil is only dissolved through love for, and service to, others.' Polly could not imagine ever losing touch with Dimpsee. Dimpsee glowed with hope.

Meadow Master opened a window for Polly on Earth where her brother George, now thirty years old, had an organic farm near Toka Mountain. Polly was astonished, 'Has that much time gone by?' With a tinge of regret, Polly thought about all the years she had missed growing up with

George. And she knew that even with her return, it could never be the same. 'But I could come back and be near him,' she thought, and the notion cheered her. Meadow Master nodded. 'Your return to Earth as the builders of this new world will ensure that out of the ashes of a dying civilization a beautiful society will grow—one based on love, justice and sharing.'

9 The World is Transformed

The students gathered, eager to participate in this new world. A window opened onto Earth. The students gasped, 'Look! It's the Black Dragon!' They stared, transfixed, as it soared through the sky towards a TV station. Circling the building, it bellowed smoke and flames. 'Oh, no!' Polly cried, 'What is happening?' Suddenly a second window flung open. It showed a television screen transmitting an interview with Meadow Master around the world.

Although the snowman looked like an ordinary man in a dark-blue pinstriped business suit and a pink shirt and silver tie, Polly could tell it was him by his eyes. The energy of love coming from Meadow Master was extraordinary. It acted like a shield to prevent any harm from occurring. There were spontaneous acts of love and kindness everywhere. Some wept tears of joy. People from around the globe were responding to Meadow Master's words.

He appeared to be speaking to everyone in their own language though he was, in fact, conveying his thoughts telepathically so that everyone understood in their heart. Even people without televisions had the same experience.

He talked about ways to solve the chaos of the world: sharing the Earth's resources, creating justice in the legal systems, ensuring health for everyone. He warned that people were being poisoned by pollution in the air, the water and the soil. Meadow Master spoke clearly and simply, "When you learn to share and consider others' needs as if they were your own, peace and kindness will prevail."

With these words, another window opened. Polly and the students saw the Black Dragon, its strength depleted, return to its cave. The dragon was powerless when confronted with the snowman's message which would free the people from fear. Meadow Master materialized behind the dragon. The Black Dragon roared in rage. It had lost.

It sent a flash of fire out of its nostrils in a futile attempt to destroy Meadow Master. But the energy of love was impenetrable and the flames recoiled, scorching the scrawny dragon. Meadow Master could not be touched by evil. The snowman master declared, "Your time has come to an end."

The Black Dragon, made of dollar bills, caught fire. Its cave, also full of paper money tainted with greed, started to burn. Flames engulfed everything. The Dragon rushed out of the cave, moaning and wailing, spreading the blaze so

that all the junk outside ignited. Eyesore Island looked like a volcanic explosion. When the fire died down, all that was left was a blanket of ashes

THE NEED & GREED YOU CAN NEVER HAVE ENOUGH UGLY IS HURT,

and a terrible silence. In the silence,
something began to move. Could the
Black Dragon be coming back to life?

Out of the intense heat of the dragon's ashes, a little
worm emerged and grew to maturity. Entranced, the
students watched.

From the worm, a bird's head burst forth, then its body
freed itself. The bird began to glow and from the ashes came
the sweet fragrance of incense. The feathers were shades of
purple and crimson with a white band around the neck and
a magnificent golden plume rising from the head. The wing
and tail feathers looked like tongues of fire. It was beautiful!
Powerful! As the bird flew upwards out of the ashes Polly
remembered the phoenix in the story her mother had read
to her. Polly shouted, 'It's a phoenix!'

The bird flew towards the Earth, its feathers absorbing
murky pollution and transforming it into light. The phoenix
wept tears of crystal light. Wherever these tears touched

the Earth, there was a new radiance. Even the stars in the sky shone with a greater brilliance. The light encompassed the students for a few moments.

They almost forgot that they were still in the valley on the Rose Planet.

Sensing that their studies were now complete, the students eagerly awaited their return to Earth. Pip had courageously decided to return to Africa. Lu was returning to a Chinese family in Tibet to bring peace and harmony there. Polly was reflective. 'My new life is prepared. My oneness with Dimpsee is my link with life on this side of the veil. Dimpsee will guide me through the many challenges ahead in my new life.'

Polly and the children were certain that their paths would be illuminated under the snowmen masters' guidance as they cooperated in building a shining future on Earth. Not only was Meadow Master now on Earth, but senior snowmen master helpers from Nada and elsewhere were now in their human bodies. Polly even saw snowmen masters on some of the white fluffy clouds as she peeped through to Earth. She saw her aging parents and the old-growth forest near Totter-Grass village still standing. Once again, Polly felt the love and warmth she had experienced with her family and friends.

Then Polly looked beneath another cloud and saw George. Her brother was running the organic farm and had married a Polynesian woman he had met at the university. They wanted to adopt a baby. 'This is my opportunity to return,' thought Polly, then hesitated. 'Is that possible?' Dimpsee shone, 'It's how we work out loving each other to the fullest.'

This changing world, growing daily in radiance, awaited Polly.

Polly took a deep breath and swung towards Earth on
her cord . . .

So ends this part of Polly's story.

May you make this adventure of transformation
your own by putting it into practice in your daily
life, as Polly will be doing.

Who will take this journey of love and
creativity? Imagine the journey to be more
beautiful than your most perfect
dream and you may be near
the truth!

The snowman glowed as stars peeped through a darkening sky.

The *Magical Master Snowman . . .*

Textile collage © 2002 Josephine Harrison, from the cover of her book "The Magical Master Snowman and the Black Dragon"
ISBN 1-894694-12-0 Published by Granville Island Publishing www.granvilleislandpublishing.com Tel 604-688-0320 Toll-free 1-877-688-0320

14″ x 19″ posters available
Photograph of original textile collage

The Magical Master Snowman

Also available from your local bookstore. *and the Black Dragon*

BOOK

CANADIAN ORDERS (For shipment in Canada – Canadian Funds)		U.S. ORDERS (For shipment to U.S. – U.S. Funds)	
___ Copies @ $14.95cdn	$_____	___ Copies @ $11.95us	$_____
Shipping (1st book)	$ 6.00cdn	Shipping (1st book)	$ 6.00us
Add $3.50cdn for each		Add $3.50us for each	
additional book	$_____	additional book	$_____
Add 7% GST	$_____		
Total Enclosed	$_____	Total Enclosed	$_____

OVERSEAS ORDERS (Outside U.S. & Canada – Payment in U.S. Funds)			
SURFACE (allow 8 weeks)		AIRMAIL	
___ Copies @ $11.95us	$_____	___ Copies @ $11.95us	$_____
Shipping (1st book)	$ 7.00us	Shipping (1st book)	$ 14.00us
Add $4.00us for each		Add $7.00us for each	
additional book	$_____	additional book	$_____
Total Enclosed	$_____	Total Enclosed	$_____

POSTER

CANADIAN ORDERS (For shipment in Canada – Canadian Funds)		U.S. ORDERS (For shipment to U.S. – U.S. Funds)	
___ Posters @ $14.95cdn	$_____	___ Posters @ $11.95us	$_____
Shipping (1st poster)	$ 6.00cdn	Shipping (1st poster)	$ 6.00us
Add $3.50cdn for each		Add $3.50us for each	
additional poster	$_____	additional poster	$_____
Add 7% GST	$_____		
Total Enclosed	$_____	Total Enclosed	$_____

OVERSEAS ORDERS (Outside U.S. & Canada – Payment in U.S. Funds)			
SURFACE (allow 8 weeks)		AIRMAIL	
___ Posters @ $11.95us	$_____	___ Posters @ $11.95us	$_____
Shipping (1st poster)	$ 7.00us	Shipping (1st poster)	$ 14.00us
Add $4.00us for each		Add $7.00us for each	
additional poster	$_____	additional poster	$_____
Total Enclosed	$_____	Total Enclosed	$_____

Make check or money order payable to Granville Island Publishing

Name _____

Address _____

City, Province/State _____

Postal/Zip Code _____

Phone (work) _____ (home)_____

Email _____

Granville Island Publishing
Suite 212–1656 Duranleau, Vancouver, BC, Canada V6H 3S4
Tel 604-688-0320 Toll-free 1-877-688-0320
www.granvilleislandpublishing.com

Thank you for your order!

Outside the church a dark shape still lurked.

Some children had gathered in the meadow near Totter-Grass that winter with the intention of building a snowman . . .

The End

and a

New Beginning